MARVEL ULTIMATE SPIDER-MAN

GREAT POWER

HEY, IT'S ME—YOUR FRIENDLY NEIGHBORHOOD SPIDER-MAN!

ADAPTED BY Michael Siglain

Based on the animated series Marvel's *Ultimate Spider-Man*

marvelkids.com

TM & © 2012 Marvel & Subs.

Printed in the United States of America

First Edition

3 5 7 9 10 8 6 4 2

G658-7729-4-12331

ISBN 978-1-4231-5476-1

SUSTAINABLE FORESTRY INITIATIVE

Certified Chain of Custody
Promoting Sustainable Forestry

www.sfiprogram.org
SFI-01415

The SFI label applies to the text stock

TURN THE PAGE AND LET'S GET GOING!

It was dawn in New York, and Spider-Man was swinging through the city. Suddenly, a police car went skidding down the street. Spidey leaped into action and fired a spiderweb, catching the car and saving the cop inside!

That's when the Trapster appeared.

The Trapster attacked at once! He threw sticky bombs at Spider-Man, but the wall-crawler used his amazing powers to jump out of the way. Then Spidey shot his webs at the Trapster, causing the villain to get stuck in his own paste!

That's when the Trapster's eyes went wide with fright. But he wasn't looking at Spider-Man, he was looking at something overhead. Something very, *very* big.

HEY, MY SPIDER-SENSE DIDN'T TINGLE! WAIT, YOU DON'T KNOW WHAT SPIDER-SENSE IS? IT'S LIKE AN ALARM CLOCK THAT WARNS ME OF DANGER. BUT WHY DIDN'T IT GO OFF NOW?

ME

Spidey looked up to see the giant S.H.I.E.L.D. Helicarrier flying above the skyscrapers of Manhattan. When Spidey turned around, he was face-to-face with Nick Fury, Director of S.H.I.E.L.D.

"Look around you, Spider-Man," Fury began. "Is this the way Captain America would've done it? Cap could've stopped Trapster in five seconds. You took three minutes, with lots of damage."

S.H.I.E.L.D. STANDS FOR THE STRATEGIC HOMELAND INTERVENTION ENFORCEMENT AND LOGISTICS DIVISION. THEY'RE THE SUPER-DUPER SPIES!

Fury looked directly at Spider-Man and made him an unbelievable offer. "I want S.H.I.E.L.D. to train you to be a better Spider-Man. The **Ultimate** Spider-Man," Fury said.

But Spidey wasn't interested. As he turned to walk away, Fury called to him. "I'm serious—Peter Parker."

Spider-Man froze in his tracks! Nick Fury knew Spider-Man's secret identity. In fact, he knew all about Spider-Man!

WHOA, DIDN'T SEE THAT ONE COMING, DID YOU? AWKWARD!

OKAY, OKAY. TURN THE PAGE.

Peter Parker had a regular childhood growing up in Queens, New York, with his Uncle Ben and Aunt May—until he was bitten by a radioactive spider. That's when he developed powers.

After his Uncle Ben died, Peter vowed to use his newfound powers for good. He created web-shooters and made a costume, and Spider-Man was born!

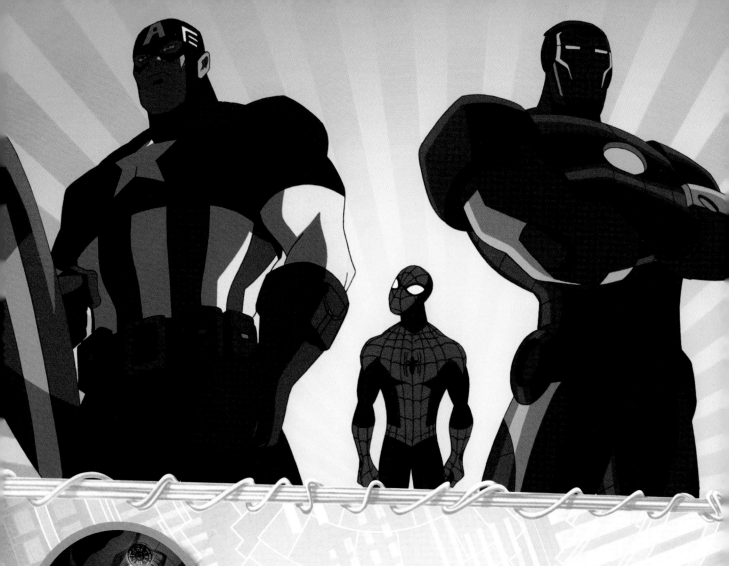

To help convince Spider-Man to join S.H.I.E.L.D., Fury gave Peter a new, high-tech web-shooter.

"With your talent and my training," Fury continued, "you can learn to be a better hero—the next Cap, the next Iron Man. One of the greats!"

Spidey thought about it. Then he realized that he was late for school.

"Thanks for the offer, but I'm not allowed to talk to strangers," Spidey said. And with that, Spider-Man fired a web and swung off, leaving Fury to wonder if the wall-crawler would even consider his offer.

mary jane

Peter got to school and immediately saw Mary Jane Watson and Harry Osborn. MJ and Harry were Peter's oldest and best friends.

HARRY OSBORN

And then there's Flash Thompson, the star athlete and resident bully of Midtown High School. Flash always picked on Peter, but Peter couldn't let Flash or anyone else at school know that he was really a Super Hero.

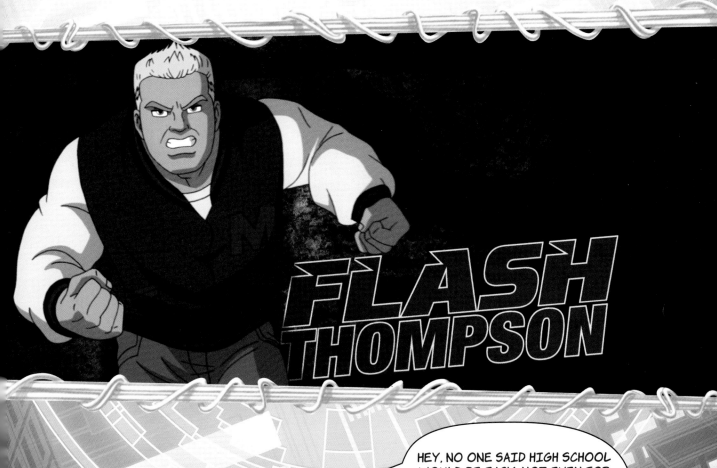

FLASH THOMPSON

HEY, NO ONE SAID HIGH SCHOOL WOULD BE EASY, NOT EVEN FOR SPIDER-MAN. BUT KEEP READING, TRUE BELIEVERS, 'CAUSE THINGS ARE ABOUT TO GET A WHOLE LOT WORSE!

While Peter was having lunch with MJ and Harry, his spider-sense started tingling like crazy. Just then, the wall on the far side of the cafeteria exploded, and the Frightful Four entered. Except there were only three of them.

"Before the Trapster was captured," the Wizard began, "he learned that Spider-Man attends this school. And unless he gives himself up, we'll tear this place down brick by brick!"

THESE GUYS = BAD NEWS.

THE WIZARD: MASTER OF HIGH-TECH GADGETS

KLAW: A VILLAIN MADE OUT OF LIVING SOUND WAVES

THUNDRA: A RUTHLESS WARRIOR WOMAN FROM ANOTHER TIMELINE—DON'T ASK!

—AND THE TRAPSTER—WAIT, I ALREADY CAUGHT HIM. . . .

Peter quickly snuck away and changed into his Spider-Man costume. He had to stop the villains and protect all the kids and teachers at school.

Spidey fired a web at Klaw and turned the villain's own sound waves against him!

Then the wall-crawler leaped off the ceiling and landed directly on Thundra. "Hey, Little Miss Muffet," Spidey called out, "the spider just kicked your tuffet!"

A TUFFET IS A BIG CUSHION THAT'S USED AS A SEAT. GO READ THE NURSERY RHYME ... I'LL WAIT.

All at once, the villains combined their powers and attacked!

Spidey had to act fast! He quickly fired a web at Klaw's hand and used the villain's sound waves against Thundra. Then the wall-crawler shot multiple webs at the Wizard and tugged hard, pulling the Wizard down into the other two Super Villains.

That's when the police arrived, allowing Spidey to rush off and change back into his school clothes.

DURING THE BATTLE, FLASH THOMPSON TOLD ME HE WAS SPIDEY'S NUMBER ONE FAN ... SO I TRICKED HIM AND MADE HIM HIDE IN A LOCKER. IT'S THE LITTLE THINGS IN LIFE THAT MAKE YOU SMILE.

The attack at the school made Peter think about Fury's offer to have S.H.I.E.L.D. train him to be a better hero.

Spider-Man was sloppy. He let himself be tracked to the high school, putting everyone in danger.

If the Super Villains ever discovered Spider-Man's secret identity, then Aunt May would be in danger.

Nick Fury was right. Spider-Man had great power, but he hadn't been using it to its full potential. He needed to be better than amazing—he needed to be ultimate—so he decided to pay Fury a visit aboard S.H.I.E.L.D.'s Helicarrier.

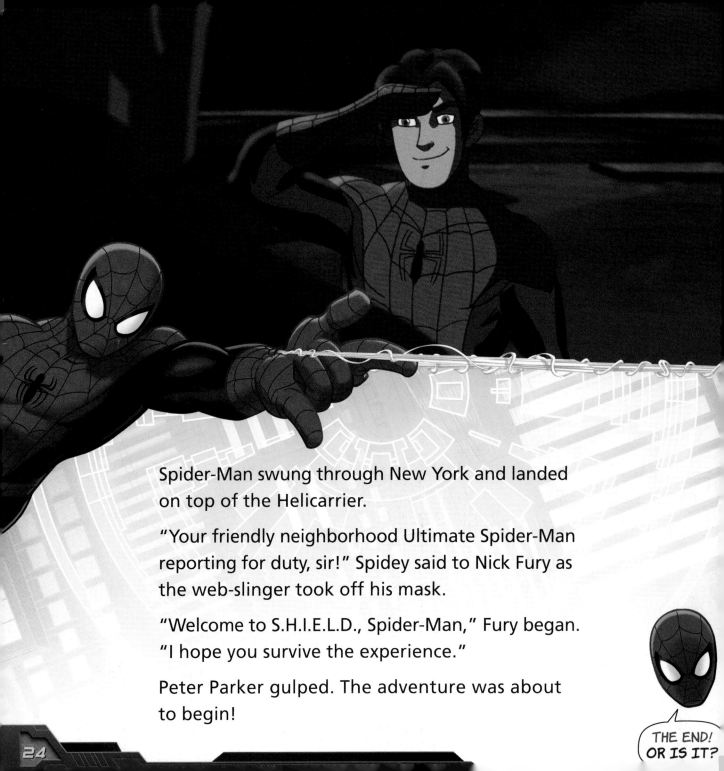

Spider-Man swung through New York and landed on top of the Helicarrier.

"Your friendly neighborhood Ultimate Spider-Man reporting for duty, sir!" Spidey said to Nick Fury as the web-slinger took off his mask.

"Welcome to S.H.I.E.L.D., Spider-Man," Fury began. "I hope you survive the experience."

Peter Parker gulped. The adventure was about to begin!

THE END! OR IS IT?